Night

Elie Wiesel

STUDENT PACKET

NOTE:

The trade book edition of the novel used to prepare this guide is found in the Novel Units catalog and on the Novel Units website. Using other editions may have varied page references.

Please note: We have assigned Interest Levels based on our knowledge of the themes and ideas of the books included in the Novel Units sets, however, please assess the appropriateness of this novel or trade book for the age level and maturity of your students prior to reading with them. You know your students best!

ISBN 978-1-56137-805-0

To order, contact your local school supply store, or:

Toll-Free Fax: 877.716.7272
Phone: 888.650.4224
3901 Union Blvd., Suite 155
St. Louis, MO 63115

sales@novelunits.com

novelunits.com

Name_____

Directions: Rate each of the following statements before you read the novel. Discuss your ratings with a partner. After you have completed the novel, rate and discuss the statements again.

1————— 2————— 3————— 4————— 5————— 6

agree strongly   strongly disagree

Before After

1. You should do what you're told.   _____ _____

2. It's better not to stick out.   _____ _____

3. What's past is past.   _____ _____

4. The Holocaust could happen again.   _____ _____

5. There is no such thing as evil; people just make mistakes.   _____ _____

6. You need to look out for yourself first.   _____ _____

7. You should never lose faith.   _____ _____

8. Parents and children shouldn't keep secrets from one another.   _____ _____

9. If someone hurts you, you should turn the other cheek.   _____ _____

10. People are amazingly resilient.   _____ _____

11. Reports of Holocaust atrocities are exaggerated.   _____ _____

12. It is harder to make independent choices when you belong to a group. _____ _____

13. No one can force you to conform.   _____ _____

14. People will always find a scapegoat.   _____ _____

15. Victims often make targets of themselves.   _____ _____

Directions: Get together in a small group. Using your pooled knowledge, see how many of the following terms and names you can identify before reading *Night.* Jot down a few notes indicating what you know, even if you have only a vague idea about the term or name. (After you have completed the novel, use what you have learned—plus additional resources if necessary—to complete the activity sheet.)

rabbi

synagogue

Kaddish

Hasidism

Talmud

Torah

Rosh Hashanah

Zionism

Maimonides

phylacteries

cabbala

Passover

Pentecost

Name_____

Directions: Freewrite (without stopping or correcting) using the following sentence-starters. Spend two or three minutes on each. (Continue on the back if you run out of space.)

1. Man's inhumanity to man...

2. Anti-Semitism today...

3. A living nightmare...

4. When something terrible happens, the idea that "It is meant to be..."

5. Feeling that you and your body are disconnected...

6. A son owes it to his father...

7. "Ethnic cleansing"...

8. Loyalty becomes fanaticism when...

Directions: Write a brief answer to each study question as you read the novel at home or in class. Use the questions for review before group discussions and before your novel test.

Pages 1-12

1. When and where was the author's early boyhood spent?

2. How was Moshe the Beadle "different"?

3. What did the author and Moshe talk about?

4. Why did Moshe disappear for a few months?

5. How did people respond to Moshe's stories about the Gestapo?

6. Why did the author's father say that he was "too old to start a new life"?

7. What happened in Sighet on the seventh day of Passover?

8. What did every Jew have to wear?

9. What was the ghetto?

10. List three rights the Jews of Sighet lost by decree.

Pages 12-20

11. Why was someone knocking on the window?

12. Why did everyone prepare to leave Sighet?

13. What did the Jews think might be the reason for their deportation?

14. List three ways the deportees were abused.

15. Where were the deportees told they were going?

Pages 21-43

16. What had "broken" Mme. Schachter?

17. What did Mme. Schachter scream about?

18. To what station were the deportees brought?

19. How did Mrs. Schachter's dream come true?

20. How did the author get separated from his mother?

21. Why didn't the deportees throw themselves on the guards?

22. What did the author see the Germans do to the truck full of children?

23. How did the author's faith change when he saw the children killed?

24. Why did the author plan to kill himself—then change his mind?

Pages 32-43

25. Who were the first ones to beat the author and the others?

26. How was everyone "disinfected"?

27. Why did the author thank God for mud?

28. What did the SS officer say would happen to those who could not work?

29. Why did the gypsy strike the author's father?

30. What advice did the Polish prisoner in charge of the block give?

31. What was tattooed on each prisoner's left arm?

32. How did the author lie to his relation from Antwerp?

33. What motto was inscribed on the plaque at Auschwitz?

34. To what new camp were Elie Wiesel and his father sent?

Name_____

Night
Study Questions
page 3

Pages 45-62

35. Why was special attention paid to some of the children at Buna?

36. Name one "job" the author had at Buna.

37. What did Yossi, Tibi, and the author plan to do after the liberation?

38. Why was the author sent to the dentist?

39. How did the French girl comfort the author?

40. Where did Wiesel and the girl meet again years later?

41. How did Franek get Wiesel to give up his gold crown?

42. Why was Wiesel given 25 lashes?

43. How were the two cauldrons of soup like "two lambs with a hundred wolves lying in wait for them"?

44. Why were the prisoners filled with joy instead of frightened by the bombs?

45. Why was the youth from Warsaw hanged?

46. Why were the Dutchman and the "pipel" hanged?

Pages 63-80

47. How many men came to the Rosh Hashanah service?

48. How was this New Year's Day different for Wiesel?

49. Why didn't Wiesel fast on Yom Kippur?

50. What "fine New Year's gift" did the SS give the Jews?

© Novel Units, Inc.

8

All rights reserved

51. What did Wiesel do to avoid "selection" by Mengele?

52. What "inheritance" did Wiesel's father give his son when the father was "selected"?

53. How did Wiesel's father avoid the second selection?

54. What did Akiba Drumer and the rabbi from Poland have in common?

55. How did Elie Wiesel end up in the hospital?

56. Why did Wiesel leave the hospital only two days after his surgery?

57. What did the head of the block have the prisoners do before moving out?

Pages 81-92
58. What made the move to Gleiwitz so hard?

59. How did Zalman die?

60. What happened to prisoners who stopped running?

61. Why did Eliezer's father make him wake up when he slept in the shed?

62. What didn't Eliezer tell Rabbi Eliahou?

63. How did Eliezer almost die in the barracks?

64. What did Juliek do before he died?

65. How did Eliezer save his father even after his father had been sent "to the left"?

Pages 93-109

66. Why was Eliezer's father almost thrown from the train?

67. How did the German workmen amuse themselves?

68. Years later, how was the Parisienne's treatment of the "natives" like the Germans' treatment of the starving Jews?

69. How did the old man and his son die?

70. How did Meir Katz save Eliezer?

71. Why did only a dozen of the original 100 prisoners get off the cattle car Eliezer was on when the train arrived in Buchenwald?

72. Why didn't Eliezer want his father to rest while he himself had a hot bath?

73. Why did Eliezer feel ashamed of himself while he searched for his father?

74. Why did Eliezer hesitate to give his sick father water?

75. Why did Eliezer hate the doctors?

76. How did the other patients treat Eliezer's father?

77. How did Eliezer's father die?

78. How much longer was Eliezer in the camp after his father died?

79. What happened when the camp resistance movement acted?

80. What was the prisoners' first concern after liberation?

81. How did Eliezer nearly die three days after the liberation?

Name_____

Night
Activity #4: Vocabulary
pages 1-20

Vocabulary List

beadle 1	Hasidic 1	synagogue 1	waiflike 1	cabbala 1
deliverance 1	Talmud 1	mysticism 2	Zohar 3	initiation 3
deportees 4	Gestapo 4	bombardment 5	rabbi 5	exterminate 6
Zionism 6	emigration 6	Fascist 6	abstraction 6	anti-Semitic 7
Passover 8	ghetto 9	Pentecost 10	firmament 10	premonition 10
haggard 11	deportation 11	edict 13	candelabra 13	phylacteries 13
truncheons 13	indiscriminately 13	convoy 14	cringing 15	portfolios 15
expelled 16	morale 18	refuge 18	guerillas 18	pillage 19

Directions: An analogy is a comparison. For example:

NO is to YES as OFF is to ON.
HILL is to MOUNTAIN as STREAM is to RIVER.

Use words from the vocabulary list above to complete the analogies, below. Then, using the back of your paper, create two analogies of your own for a partner to solve.

1. THEATER is to ENTERTAINMENT as _____ is to SAFETY.

2. RACIST is to PEOPLE OF COLOR as _____ is to JEWS.

3. IMMOBILIZATION is to FIX as _____ is to CARRY OFF.

4. NURTURE is to SUSTAIN as KILL is to _____.

5. SELF-GOVERNING is to DEMOCRATIC as DICTATORIAL is to_____.

6. COMING is to IMMIGRATION as GOING is to _____.

7. KGB is to RUSSIAN as _____ is to NAZI.

8. SWITCHBLADES are to CUT as _____ are to BEAT.

Name_____

Vocabulary List

constraint 21	hermetically 22	pious 22	abyss 23	barometer 24
abominable 25	tommy gun 27	sages 29	monocle 29	unremittingly 29
crematory 30	lorry 30	Kaddish 31	infernal 31	barracks 32
antechamber 32	bestial 32	lucidity 34	redemption 34	petrol 34
oppressive 35	harangued 36	leprous 36	convalescent 36	colic 36
clout 37	compulsory 38	siesta 39	veteran 39	wizened 40
humane 41	blandishments 43			

Directions: Complete each sentence by choosing the word from the vocabulary list that best fits. Write the word on the blank line.

1. She was an extremely _____ person who dedicated her life to relieving the suffering of others.

2. The drill sergeant _____ the new recruits, scolding them for a half hour about their sloppy appearance and poorly made beds.

3. The dead woman's family drove with the urn from the _____ to the lake, where they scattered her ashes.

4. She tried flattery and coaxing, but her _____ left him unmoved.

5. The escaped political prisoner described the _____ treatment she had received at the hands of her savage torturers.

6. The _____ rumbled through the streets of London with its load of bricks.

7. Lord Periwinkle gasped in surprise and the _____ popped from his eye.

8. You do not have to attend batting practice on Thursday, but the Saturday practice is _____.

9. She tried standing on her head, breathing into a bag, and holding her breath, but the hiccups continued _____.

10. The hiker needed food that wouldn't spoil, so she bought packages of dried fruit that had been _____ sealed.

12

Name_____

Directions: Answer the following questions by circling the letter in the YES or NO column. Then put the letters in the blanks to find why Elie Wiesel did not weep when his father died.

	YES	NO
1. Were the Three Stooges **buffoons**?	H	S
2. Would you like to be a source of **derision**?	O	E
3. Would a **din** hurt your eyes?	R	H
4. Would **dysentery** give you a stomach ache?	A	R
5. Is a heavy backpack an **encumbrance**?	D	O
6. Would a loner appreciate some **privations**?	H	N
7. Would you find a **tether** around an animal's neck?	O	W
8. Should you apply brakes **spasmodically** on slippery pavement?	M	L
9. Could you eat **rations**?	O	N
10. Could a **tempest** cause trees to fall?	R	A
11. Would you find **automatons** in an engine?	Z	E
12. Could you find passengers in a **queue**?	T	I
13. Would **liquidation** of a camp produce a pool of drinking water?	H	E
14. Has a **bereaved** husband lost his wife?	A	I
15. Is crying a sign of **apathy**?	T	R
16. Would a typical condemned prisoner want a **reprieve**?	S	L

___ ___ ___ ___ ___ ___ ___ ___ ___ ___ ___ ___ ___ ___ ___ ___
1   2   3   4   5   6   7   8   9 10 11   12 13 14 15 16

Name_____

Directions: Wiesel tells us that before Dr. Mengele conducted one "selection," some of the younger men tried to incite the others to try overpowering the guards (page 29). Think about the arguments for and against revolting.

With a partner, take turns jotting in the **YES** and **NO** columns the pros and cons of turning on the armed SS officers. It is okay to write down key words and phrases rather than whole sentences. Try to include as many reasons under "YES" as you do under "NO." Discuss your chart with another pair of partners and try to reach consensus (agreement) on whether or not the group ended up making the best decision. A spokesperson for this group of four then reports the group-of-four's conclusion to the whole class. Dissenting views are heard at this time.

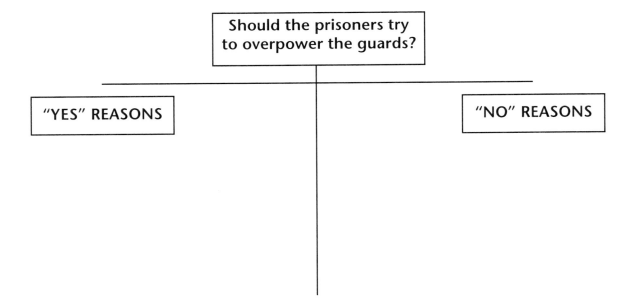

Should the prisoners try to overpower the guards?

"YES" REASONS   "NO" REASONS

The reason that best supports the group's conclusion is:

On a separate sheet of paper, write an essay in which you defend or criticize the group's decision to continue their march rather than revolt. Use some of the ideas from the prewriting chart, above, to support your argument.

Name_____

Directions: One helpful strategy when making a difficult decision is to think of as many alternatives as possible, then evaluate each one. The "yardsticks" used to measure each possible solution are called **criteria**. The criteria in the chart below are phrased as questions.

In 1944, the Jews of Sighet face some difficult choices based on limited information. *What should they do about the threat posed to their families by Hitler?*

Analyze their choices at this point by (a) adding two more choices to those already listed in the chart below; (b) adding another criterion; and (c) scoring each decision: 1=yes, 2=maybe, or 3=no.

Possible Choices ↓	Criteria			
	Will we avoid having to "start all over"?	Will we be safe from Hitler?	Will we be allowed to practice our religion?	
Stay in Sighet and change nothing.				
Emigrate to Palestine.				
Try to "pass" as an Aryan.				

On your grid, which alternative received the greatest total number of points? _____ Was this the alternative Wiesel's family chose?_____ Why did Wiesel's father think his decision was the best one?

Writing Activity: Write an interior monologue revealing Eliezer's thoughts as he tries to convince his father to emigrate to Palestine.

Name_____   *Night*

Project: Write a poem about the changes that Eliezer undergoes during his time in the concentration camps.

Directions:
1. Reread pages 1-3, describing a time before the camps and pages 107-109, after the liberation.
2. Discuss with a partner how Eliezer changed—physically, spiritually, emotionally.
3. Jot down a list of hopes, pleasures, desires, plans that Eliezer used to have.
4. Jot down how Eliezer feels about his former plans and his loss of faith.
5. If you like, choose a line or two of prose from the book and incorporate it into your poem. (See the sample, below.)
6. Proceed to write the poem using the following format. (Vary that format however you wish.)

Once, New Year's Day had dominated my life   (page 64)
Now I had ceased to plead, to plead

Once, _____

Now, _____

Once, _____

Now, _____

Once, _____

Now, _____

Once, _____

Now, _____

7. Read your poem aloud and rework it in any way you choose. Are there unnecessary words? Would you like to vary the once/now format? Are there other images you would like to add? Have you shown your reader what you mean?

8. Choose a title: _____

ACROSS

2. Wiesel didn't do this on Yom Kippur.
5. Disease which killed Wiesel's father
7. Concentration camp where Wiesel endured Idek's attacks
8. Systematic extermination of European Jews by Nazis
10. Wiesel begged his father to take the family here.
15. Concentration camp in Germany from which Wiesel was freed
17. The Jews were crowded into ____ cars.
19. Concentration camp in Poland where Wiesel was first taken
23. What the author's family called him
25. Notorious doctor who wrote down names for selection
26. Section of city where Jews were required to live

DOWN

1. Wiesel found a poor foreign Jew to guide him in his studies of this.
3. Every Jew had to wear a _____ star.
4. The Nazis used needles to ___numbers on prisoners' arms.
6. Town in Transylvania where the Wiesels lived
9. Process of deciding who was to die next
11. Wiesel lost this because of its gold crown.
12. Jewish prisoners were not allowed to play music by these composers.
13. Prayer for the dead
14. German state secret police during Nazi regime
15. Nobody believed Moshe the _____.
16. The French girl passed herself off as ___.
18. Furnace for burning bodies
20. Schutzstaffel Troops; Hitler's special police force
21. Rosh ____marks the beginning of the Jewish New Year.
22. Adolf____, Nazi dictator of Germany
24. Movement to create a national Jewish homeland

Name_____

True/False: Mark each statement T or F.

___ 1. Elie Wiesel grew up in Germany.

___ 2. Wiesel's father was a shopkeeper.

___ 3. Wiesel's father encouraged him to study the cabbala.

___ 4. Moshe the Beadle guided Wiesel in his studies of the cabbala.

___ 5. Moshe the Beadle barely escaped death at the hands of the Gestapo.

___ 6. The Jews prepared to flee from Sighet when Moshe the Beadle described the extermination he had witnessed.

___ 7. The Germans set up two ghettos in Sighet surrounded by barbed wire.

___ 8. The Jews of Sighet were deported by cattle car.

___ 9. Madame Schachter screamed about a fire no one could see.

___ 10. Only Madame Schachter could see the flames coming from the chimneys at Auschwitz.

___ 11. Wiesel's sister and mother fled to safety in Palestine.

___ 12. Wiesel saw children thrown into the flames.

___ 13. Those who could not work were sent to the infirmary.

___ 14. Prisoners had their names tattooed on their ankles.

___ 15. Some of the veteran prisoners beat the new ones.

Matching: Match each cause with its effect.

Causes

___ 16. Wiesel wanted to give his relative good news about his wife and sons.

___ 17. Foreign Jews were ordered out of Sighet.

___ 18. Jews were ordered to hand over valuables or die.

___ 19. Madame Schacter kept screaming.

___ 20. Flesh was burning.

Effects

A. Wiesel's father buried the family savings.

B. The prisoners noticed a pestilential stench in the air when they stopped at Auschwitz.

C. He described a pleasant visit he remembered.

D. Other prisoners tied her up.

E. Wiesel's father stuffed money into his boot.

F. Moshe the Beadle was expelled.

G. He lied to Stein.

H. German guards beat her.

Name_____

Fill-Ins: Fill in each blank with the word, name, or phrase that makes the statement true.

1._____ ("Eliezer" to his family) grew up in the town of Sighet in Transylvania. The only son of shopkeeper parents, he was the third of four children. In 1941 when Wiesel was 12 he spent a lot of time with Moshe the Beadle, who guided him in 2._____. One day he and all the other foreign Jews were 3._____. When he returned several months later people refused 4. _____. He described how the foreign Jews had been sent to Poland and systematically 5. _____. Wounded in the leg, Moshe was taken for dead and managed to escape. In the Spring of 1944, the townspeople of Sighet were optimistic that 6._____ would soon be defeated. Wiesel failed to persuade his father to sell out and emigrate with the family to 7. _____. Then 8._____ soldiers suddenly appeared in Sighet. A week later the leaders of the Jewish community were 9._____ and Jews were ordered not to leave their houses. Three days later every Jew was told to wear a 10._____star. Next, two 11._____ were set up, surrounded by barbed wire. Finally, the Gestapo gave the deportation order and the Jews were crammed into 12._____ _____,eighty people per car. Madame Schachter, a woman with a young 13._____, lost her mind and began screaming at intervals about the 14._____ that only she could see. The train reached Birkenau, the reception center for 15._____ —and there were the flames for all to see, rising from tall chimneys.

Short Answer: For each question, write a brief but concise answer of one or two complete sentences.

16.   When was the last time Elie Wiesel saw his mother and sister?

17.   Whom did Wiesel see taken from a truck and thrown into the flames?

18.   Describe the incident where Wiesel considered suicide—but decided against it.

19.   Who were the "Kapos" and how did they treat the newcomers?

20.   What item of clothing did Wiesel manage to keep?

21.   How did Wiesel become "A-7713"?

22.   What sort of lie did Wiesel tell his relative, Stein—and why?

Name_____

Identification: Find a character in the box who matches the description on the left. Write the letter of the character next to the matching number. Each character is to be used only once.

A.	Eliezer
B.	Tzipora
C.	Mr. Wiesel
D.	Mme. Schachter
E.	Dr. Mengele
F.	Akiba Drumer
G.	Juliek
H.	Idek
I.	Rabbi Eliahou
J.	Meir Katz
K.	Adolf Hitler

____ 1. The notorious Nazi who wrote down Mr. Wiesel's number.

____ 2. The frenzy-prone Kapo who beat Wiesel in the warehouse.

____ 3. She lost her mind and screamed about fire.

____ 4. He played his violin the night he died.

____ 5. This powerful man saved Wiesel from being strangled.

____ 6. Wiesel hoped he wouldn't desert his father, like this man's son did.

____ 7. This is what the author's family called him.

____ 8. A cultured shopkeeper, he was "more concerned with others than with his own family."

____ 9. When he lost his faith, he died and the others forgot to say Kaddish as they had promised.

____ 10. This younger sister of the author disappeared with her mother.

____ 11. The Jews of Sighet doubted at first that he was really planning to exterminate Jews around the globe

Multiple Choice: To the left of each item number, write the letter of the BEST response.

____ 12. The narrator of *Night* is
    A. an objective, omniscient narrator
    B. Elie Wiesel
    C. a survivor who knew Wiesel

___ 13. The narrator describes which of the following time periods?
A. 1914-1917, when Wiesel was in his twenties
B. 1923-1926, when Wiesel was a pre-teen
C. 1943-1946, when Wiesel was a teenager

___ 14. Elie Wiesel's family probably would have avoided the concentration camps if they had
A. refused to get into the cattle car
B. bribed the SS officers instead of burying their money
C. fled to Palestine when Moshe warned them

___ 15. When Wiesel first saw children murdered at Birkenau, he
A. prayed for the Lord's protection from death
B. rebelled against a Lord who would allow this to happen
C. told himself this must be part of the Lord's plan

___ 16. "Never shall I forget that _____, the first ____ in camp, which has turned my life into one long _____"
A. dream, dream, dream
B. day, day, day
C. night, night, night

___ 17. Elie Wiesel hoped that he would pass the test better than Rabbi Eliahou's son had. In other words, Wiesel hoped he would
A. not desert his father
B. carry out his father's wishes that he become a rabbi
C. never turn his own father in

___ 18. An SS officer announced that those who _____ would die in the furnaces.
A. could not work
B. wore yellow stars
C. had numbers on their arms

___ 19. The young Pole and others who stole food during air raid alerts were
A. hanged
B. given reduced rations
C. beaten

___ 20. When thousands attended a Rosh Hashanah service in the camp, Wiesel
A. fasted
B. did not join the prayers
C. spoke the blessing

___ 21. Wiesel had an operation on his
A. foot
B. hand
C. eye

___ 22. If Wiesel had remained in the hospital, he would probably soon have been
A. exterminated
B. liberated
C. the subject of experimentation

___ 23. After playing a Beethoven concerto in the barracks, Juliek
A. gave his violin to Wiesel
B. was beaten for playing German music
C. died

___ 24. Wiesel saw German workmen laugh as prisoners fought to the death over
A. a gold coin
B. a game of cards
C. a crust of bread

___ 25. What did the French girl, Meir Katz, and Elie Wiesel's father all have in common?
A. They all stood silently by when Elie Wiesel was attacked.
B. They all tried to help Elie Wiesel.
C. They each met Elie Wiesel again years later in France.

___ 26. The main reason Wiesel didn't want to give his father drinking water was
A. he wanted to drink the water himself
B. water would make his dysentery worse
C. he was looking forward to using the water for a bath

___ 27. When his father died, Elie Wiesel
A. carried the body to the crematory
B. lit candles in his memory
C. woke to find his father had been taken away

___ 28. When the prisoners were finally liberated from Buchenwald, their first thought was of
A. revenge
B. their families
C. food

___ 29. Which of the following is NOT a major theme developed in *Night*?
A. the power of optimism
B. man's inhumanity to man
C. the loss of faith

___ 30. Which of the following best describes the tone at the end of *Night:* "The look in his eyes, as they stared into mine, has never left me"?
A. anguish, emptiness
B. soothing, relief
C. uplifting, optimism

___ 31. Which of the following best expresses Elie Wiesel's primary purpose in writing *Night*?
A. To remember the good people who helped him.
B. To forgive the Nazis and heal old wounds.
C. To make sure that such horrors will never happen again.

Identification: In one or two complete sentences, explain who each person or group was.

1. Eliezer

2. Tzipora

3. Mr. Wiesel

4. Mme. Schachter

5. Dr. Mengele

6. SS Officers

7. Kapos

8. Rabbi Eliahou and his son

9. Adolf Hitler

10. Tibi and Yossi

Short Answer: Answer each question in one or two complete sentences.

11. What do you suppose was the most frightening moment for Elie Wiesel?

12. Describe at least three types of physical suffering Elie Wiesel and the other prisoners were forced to undergo.

13. Describe one incident where the Germans obviously enjoyed the prisoners' suffering.

14. Describe a situation in the book where someone risked his or her life to help someone else.

15. Describe a situation in the book where one or more prisoners became victims of other prisoners.

16. Describe one piece of evidence from the book that the Germans victimized children.

17. Describe one piece of evidence from the book that those who were too weak to work were killed.

18. Describe one instance where passivity prevented Jews from protecting themselves from Hitler.

19. Cite one instance where Elie Wiesel describes the inmates as acting like animals—and explain what he means.

20. Cite one instance where Elie Wiesel describes those in charge of the camp as acting like animals—and explain what he means.

21. Cite one piece of evidence that Elie Wiesel lost some of his religious faith while in the camps.

Essay

I. **Analysis**
   Directions: Select A, B, or C and indicate on your paper the letter of the question you decide to answer.

   A. Support or contradict the following statement about Elie Wiesel based on *Night*. Be sure to use at least three pieces of evidence from the book to support your view: *Eliezer probably would not have survived life in the camps if he had been alone, without his father.*

   B. What did you learn about the Holocaust—that you never knew before—by reading *Night*? Why is what you learned important to you?

   C. Compare and contrast the experiences of two teenagers you have "met" through Holocaust literature—Elie Wiesel and _____ (e.g., Anne Frank—*Diary of a Young Girl*; Ellen Rosen—*Number the Stars*). (Indicate the character and novel you are using for comparison and contrast.)

II. **Critical/Creative Writing**
   Directions: Select D, E, or F.

   D. Respond to the following statement by a fictional teacher.
   "I realize that *Night* is a powerful, well-written book but I would not use it in class. I would prefer to have students read a more uplifting piece of Holocaust literature, such as *The Diary of a Young Girl* by Anne Frank or Lois Lowry's *Number the Stars*." Include at least three reasons why you do or do not support the teacher's opinion.

   E. Choose any point in the book. Write three journal entries about that episode—one that might have been made by Elie Wiesel, one by his father, and one by an SS officer. (For example, what might each have written in his journal the first night at Auschwitz?)

   F. Robert McAfee Brown states in the preface that there are many people who would prefer to believe that Wiesel's story is not true. Indeed, many "revisionist" sites have been set up on the Internet. Based on what you have learned from *Night*, write a letter of response to those who claim that the atrocities never happened—or were exaggerated.

27

Answer Key

Activities #1, #2, #3 are open-ended. Allow time for discussion in pairs, small group, or whole group.

Study Guide

1- Sighet, Transylvania—Hungary; 1930s and 40s.
2- He was a poor, foreign Jew, timid, knowledgeable about mysticism.
3- the cabbala
4- Foreign Jews were deported, slaughtered by the Gestapo in Poland.
5- They didn't believe him.
6- His son tried to convince him to flee to Palestine.
7- Germans arrested leaders of the Jewish community.
8- a yellow star
9- fenced-in area where Jews were forced to live
10- right to keep valuables in their homes, right to leave their houses, right to enter restaurants, cafes, travel by rail, attend synagogue, go out after 6:00
11- It was probably an inspector in the Hungarian police warning his friend, Mr. Wiesel, of danger.
12- The Germans gave a deportation order.
13- Some thought the deportation was for their own good because the front was close—or because Germans feared the Jews would help the guerillas.
14- forced to relieve themselves in the synagogue, sealed tight in cattle cars, threatened with death if they tried to flee, ordered to run with heavy packs, denied water
15- The destination was kept secret
16- She had been separated from her husband and two eldest sons.
17- a fire no one else could see
18- Birkenau—reception center for Auschwitz
19- At Birkenau, the prisoners saw flames from the ovens.
20- Women and children were ordered to the right and killed.
21- Some of the younger ones wanted to, but the older ones told them not to lose faith.
22- He saw the Germans throw the children into the flames.
23- He felt revolt against a Lord who could allow this to happen rise within him.
24- He thought he was destined for the flames anyway, but orders came at the last minute to go to a barracks.
25- other prisoners with truncheons
26- by soaking in petrol
27- Because his shoes were mud-covered, they were overlooked.
28- They would go into the furnace.
29- He had a stomach ache, asked to go to the lavatory.
30- Keep courage, faith, help one another
31- a number
32- He told his relative his mother had had news from Stein's family—so that Stein wouldn't worry about the truth, that they hadn't been heard from in a few years.
33- Work is liberty.
34- Buna

35- There was traffic in homosexuals among many Germans.
36- working in an electrical equipment warehouse counting bolts and fittings
37- take the first boat to Haifa
38- to have his gold crown removed and confiscated
39- After his beating, she gave him bread, told him not to cry.
40- in Paris, in the Metro
41- Franek tormented Wiesel's father.
42- He laughed when he saw Idek with a young girl.
43- Prisoners were not allowed to touch the unattended soup and would be killed for "stealing" any during the air raid.
44- They hoped the Germans would be defeated.
45- He "stole" during the alert.
46- The adult and the boy under him supposedly helped sabotage the power station.
47- Ten thousand men came to the service.
48- He used to believe profoundly; now he felt that he was God's accuser.
49- His father didn't want him to weaken himself; also his faith was shaken.
50- selection of some for the crematory
51- ran quickly, kept his left arm from showing
52- a spoon and knife
53- He convinced the Germans he could still be useful.
54- Both lost their faith—and subsequently, their lives.
55- He needed an operation for a swollen, infected foot.
56- Evacuation was ordered; he was afraid all the weakened patients would be killed.
57- clean the wooden floor
58- It was dark, very cold; prisoners were not allowed to rest.
59- He was trampled when he fell.
60- They were shot.
61- He didn't want his son to slip into unconsciousness in the cold.
62- The son he was looking for had deliberately deserted him.
63- He was nearly suffocated by the crowd of prisoners.
64- played a piece of Beethoven's concerto
65- Eliezer ran after his father, created confusion in the midst of which both returned to the "right."
66- Orders had been given for corpses to be thrown out and the father was very weak.
67- They tossed a bit of bread into the crowd of prisoners.
68- The woman enjoyed watching children at Aden fight each other for coins she tossed.
69- They and others fought for bread.
70- He pulled off someone who was trying to strangle the sleeping Wiesel.
71- The others had died.
72- He was afraid his father would die in the cold.
73- He had left his father without troubling himself.
74- Water would only make his dysentery worse.
75- They wouldn't help his father, wanted to finish off the sick.
76- They hit him since he couldn't go outside to relieve himself.

77- An SS officer hit him in the head with a truncheon when he asked repeatedly for water.
78- His father died in January; Eliezer left Buchenwald in April.
79- The SS fled and the resistance took charge.
80- getting food
81- He was hospitalized with food poisoning.

Activity #4: 1-refuge; 2-anti-Semitic; 3-deportation; 4-exterminate; 5-Fascist; 6-emigration; 7-Gestapo; 8-truncheons; Students provide two analogies of their own.
Activity #5: 1-humane; 2-harangued; 3-crematory; 4-blandishments; 5-bestial; 6-lorry; 7-monocle; 8-compulsory; 9-unremittingly; 10-hermetically
Activity #6: HE HAD NO MORE TEARS.
Activity #7: Answers will vary. Reasons YES should include—possibility of overpowering the officers, saving others; reasons NO should include possibility of getting killed, risking retribution against others.
Activity #8: Answers will vary. While some students may criticize the Jews of Sighet for passivity, others might point out that we view the situation now "with the certainty of hindsight."
Activity #9: Personal response.
Activity #10: Crossword solution is on last page.

Comprehension Quiz, Level I
True/False: 1-F; 2-T; 3-F; 4-T; 5-T; 6-F; 7-T; 8-T; 9-T; 10-F; 11-F; 12-T; 13-F; 14-F; 15-T
Matching: 16-G; 17-F; 18-A; 19-D; 20-B

Comprehension Quiz, Level II
Fill-Ins: (Accept similar answers.) 1-Elie Wiesel; 2-his studies of the cabbala; 3-expelled from Sighet; 4-to believe his terrible story; 5-slaughtered by the Gestapo; 6-Germany; 7-Palestine; 8-German; 9-arrested; 10-yellow; 11-ghettos; 12-cattle wagons; 13-son; 14-fire; 15-Auschwitz
Short Answer: 16-Elie Wiesel last saw his mother and sister when they first entered the concentration camp and were ordered "to the right"—and sent to the ovens. 17-Wiesel saw a truckload of children thrown into the flames. 18-Wiesel considered running into the electric barbed wire rather than being sent into the flames, but at the last minute the group of men was ordered into a barracks. 19-The Kapos were prisoners in charge of each barracks who beat the newcomers. 20-Wiesel managed to keep his muddy shoes. 21-Each prisoner had a number tattooed on his arm. 22-He told Stein a reassuring lie about hearing from Stein's wife and daughters so that Stein wouldn't worry about them.

Novel Test, Level I
Identification: 1-E; 2-H; 3-D; 4-G; 5-J; 6-I; 7-A; 8-C; 9-F; 10-B; 11-K
Multiple Choice: 12-B; 13-C; 14-C; 15-B; 16-C; 17-A; 18-A; 19-A; 20-B; 21-A; 22-B; 23-C; 24-C; 25-B; 26-B; 27-C; 28-C; 29-A; 30-A; 31-C

Novel Test, Level II
Identification:

1- "Eliezer" was the family's name for Elie Wiesel, the Holocaust survivor who tells his story in *Night*.
2- Tzipora was Wiesel's little sister, sent to the ovens with his mother.
3- Mr. Wiesel was Elie Wiesel's shopkeeper father. The two kept together as they were moved from camp to camp, but Wiesel's father died before the liberation.
4- Mme. Schachter was a Jew from Sighet who lost her mind in the cattle car on the way to Auschwitz and screamed about the flames only she could see.
5- Dr. Mengele was an infamous Nazi who "selected" Wiesel's father at one point.
6- SS officers were members of Hitler's special police force.
7- Kapos were appointed heads of concentration camp barracks—prisoners themselves.
8- Rabbi Eliahou searched for the son who—unbeknownst to him, but observed by Elie Wiesel—had deliberately left his father behind.
9- Adolf Hitler was the Nazi dictator of Germany whose plan it was to exterminate Jews and others in the creation of a "pure" Aryan race.
10- Tibi and Yossi were brothers—whose parents had been exterminated—befriended by Elie Wiesel in the concentration camp.

Short Answer

11- Answers will vary. Sample: He was probably terrified as he approached the crematory at Birkenau, thinking he was about to be burned alive.
12- Sample: They were starved, beaten, made to march in freezing temperatures, humiliated.
13- Sample: Germans laughed as prisoners ate snow from each others' backs and fought over bread.
14- Sample: Members of the camp resistance organization decided to prevent the liquidation of Jews at Buchenwald; Meir Katz pulled off the man who tried to strangle Elie Wiesel.
15- Sample: The veteran prisoners beat the newcomers to Auschwitz; Kapos demanded gold fillings, shoes.
16- Sample: Wiesel himself was a child when he experienced abuse by the Nazis; Wiesel saw children thrown into the flames of the ovens
17- Veteran prisoners and SS officers told Wiesel those who couldn't work would be "selected" and killed; Wiesel himself saw weak old men whose numbers were called disappear.
18- Sample: The Jews of Sighet could have fled when Moshe told his story, but they didn't believe him; Wiesel's father refused to flee to Palestine.
19- Sample: He describes the inmates fighting over bread as beasts of prey; they were responding to bestial hunger and had lost their compassion for each other.
20- Sample: Wiesel compares the German head of the tent to a wolf and describes the man's sexual interest in the children.
21- Sample: He did not pray with the others on Rosh Hashanah and rebelled against a God who could allow children to be murdered.

Essay

I. A. Students who support the statement might point out that Wiesel's father kept him from sleeping too long in the snow, called out for help when his son was being strangled, gave his son a reason to live. **B.** Personal response. **C.** Answers will vary.

II. D. Students who support the statement might point out that reading this story is a painful journey—and that the book ends on a bleak note. Students who contradict the statement might argue that there was much that was unremittingly evil about the Holocaust—and that we need to address such depressing subject matter directly if we are to ensure that such atrocities never happen again. **E.** Personal Response. **F.** Personal Response. (Students who choose F should point out that Wiesel was an eyewitness to some of the atrocities that revisionists deny—such as killing of babies, "selection" and killing of those too weak to work.)